INDIANA JONES
AND THE
SPEAR OF DESTINY

PART TWO

SCRIPT & COLORS
Elaine Lee

ART
Dan Spiegle

LETTERS
Carrie Spiegle

COVER ART
Hugh Fleming

Spotlight

DARK HORSE COMICS

VISIT US AT
www.abdopublishing.com

Reinforced library bound edition published in 2009 by Spotlight, a division of the ABDO Publishing Group, 8000 West 78th Street, Edina, Minnesota 55439. Spotlight produces high-quality reinforced library bound editions for schools and libraries. Published by agreement with Dark Horse Comics, Inc., and Lucasfilm Ltd.

Library of Congress Cataloging-in-Publication Data

Lee, Elaine.
  Indiana Jones and the Spear of Destiny / Elaine Lee, script, colors ; Will Simpson, pencils ; Dan Spiegle, inks ; Clem Robins, letters ; Hugh Fleming, cover art ; Teena Gores, publication design ; Bob Cooper & Dan Thorsland, edits. -- Reinforced library bound ed.
      p. cm. -- (Indiana Jones)
  "Dark Horse."
  ISBN 978-1-59961-578-3 (vol. 2)
  1. Graphic novels. [1. Graphic novels.] I. Simpson, Will, ill. II. Title.
  PZ7.7.L44In 2008
  [Fic]--dc22

                                                            2008009794

All Spotlight books have reinforced library bindings and are manufactured in the United States of America.